The Pu

Piper's First Show

Susan Hughes

illustrated by
Leanne Franson

Scholastic Canada Ltd.

Toronto New York London Auckland Sydney
Mexico City New Delhi Hong Kong Buenos Aires

Scholastic Canada Ltd.
604 King Street West, Toronto, Ontario M5V 1E1, Canada

Scholastic Inc.
557 Broadway, New York, NY 10012, USA

Scholastic Australia Pty Limited
PO Box 579, Gosford, NSW 2250, Australia

Scholastic New Zealand Limited
Private Bag 94407, Botany, Manukau 2163, New Zealand

Scholastic Children's Books
Euston House, 24 Eversholt Street, London NW1 1DB, UK

www.scholastic.ca

Library and Archives Canada Cataloguing in Publication
Hughes, Susan, 1960-, author
Piper's first show / Susan Hughes ; illustrated by Leanne Franson.
(The puppy collection ; 5)
ISBN 978-1-4431-3360-9 (pbk.)
I. Franson, Leanne, illustrator II. Title.
III. Series: Hughes, Susan, 1960-. The puppy collection ; 5
PS8565.U42P57 2015   jC813'.54   C2014-904506-9

Thank you to Dr. Stephanie Avery, DVM, for her puppy exertise.

Cover Credits:
Cover: Bernese © PHOTOCREO Michal Bednarek/Shutterstock;
Jewel border: olia_nikolina/Fotolia.com.
Logo: © Mat Hayward/Shutterstock.com; © Michael Pettigrew/Shutterstock.com;
© Picture-Pets/Shutterstock.com. Background: © Anne Precious/Shutterstock.com.
Back cover: pendant © Little Wale/Shutterstock.com.

6 5 4 3 2 1   Printed in Canada 121   15 16 17 18 19

MIX
Paper from
responsible sources
FSC® C004071
www.fsc.org

*For adorable Jovan Thanh Ho and
his pal Summit*

CHAPTER ONE

There were ten puppies — no, maybe twenty! They were all sitting in a row, looking up at Kat. Some were grey, some were white, some were brown. One was black with a white tail. One was white with a black tail. They all had sparkling eyes. They all looked up at Kat hopefully.

Kat was standing in the schoolyard near the gate. She was leaning against the oak tree. Her eyes were closed. She was waiting for her best friend Maya.

"Pick one, Katherine!" said Kat's father. He swept his arm out. "Pick your favourite puppy. Your mother and I have changed our minds. We want you to have a puppy of your very own!"

A puppy of her very own! But how could she pick just one?

"Kat?" a voice called. "Hey, Kat!"

Kat kept her eyes closed. It was a chilly autumn afternoon, but she didn't want to move. She didn't want her daydream to end. It was her favourite one in the world. In real life, her parents would not allow her to get a puppy. They said they didn't have enough time to look after one.

There was a red Irish setter sitting next to a gangly Great Dane puppy. There was a curly-haired cinnamon poodle beside a silky-haired golden retriever pup. A cocker spaniel puppy with floppy ears sat next to a Boston terrier pup with upright ears.

They were all just so sweet! And they were all looking up at her, waiting.

"Hey, Kat." The voice was hard to ignore. It was right beside her now. "Kat-nip! Wakey-wakey!"

Kat's eyes shot open. It was her best friend Maya, of course. She was the only one who could get away with calling her Kat-nip. Maya thought it was funny that a girl who loved dogs so much was called Kat, short for Katherine. She liked to tease Kat about it. Often Kat teased her back. It was okay because she and Maya had been best friends forever. They couldn't remember a time they didn't know each other. They had gone to the same nursery school. They had played soccer together and taken swimming lessons together. They didn't like to do exactly the same things, but they did share many interests. And the most important one was dogs. Maya loved dogs as much as Kat did.

"Kat-nip? Done with daydreaming for now?"

Maya said, with a grin. "I thought your Aunt Jenn wanted us to come right after school. You did say there is a puppy waiting for us at Tails Up. So, any time you're ready . . ."

"Okay, okay, I'm ready!" Kat said, making a face at Maya. "Come on. Let's go!"

Tails Up! Grooming and Boarding was the dog-grooming salon owned by Kat's aunt. She had opened it just a short time ago. It had been a success since the very first day. Recently, Aunt Jenn had hired a receptionist. But she still needed extra help when puppies came to stay overnight. That's when she counted on Kat and Kat's friends Maya and Grace to lend a hand.

"Where's Grace?" Maya asked, as they headed to the salon. "Isn't she coming?"

"She's going to meet us there," explained Kat. "She had to drop some books at the library first."

When the girls came to the main street of Orchard Valley, they turned the corner and

headed along the sidewalk. They hurried past
a restaurant, the barber shop, the bank and
several stores.

When they got to Tails Up, they saw Grace
waiting outside. She was breathing hard.

"I ran to the library and then to here," she
explained, with a grin. "I didn't want to miss
anything!"

Kat smiled at her. Grace was dog crazy too!

The bell on the front door jingled as they pushed it open and went inside.

Tony, the receptionist, looked up from behind the front desk. "Hello, ladies," he said. "Jenn should be out in a minute."

Aunt Jenn was so busy grooming dogs, she didn't have time to answer the phones or make appointments. Tony took care of all that now. Tony had a fifteen-year-old tabby cat, Marmalade. She went everywhere with him. She sat high up on the counter and looked down on all the dogs that came and went.

"Hi, Tony," the girls replied.

"How are you today, Marmalade?" Kat added. The girls stroked the elderly cat. She pretended she didn't care, but she purred loudly.

"As always, snobby on the outside and a marshmallow on the inside," Tony said, with a grin. Then the phone rang and he turned to answer it.

There were two customers in the waiting room. An elderly man sat on the couch with a shaggy German shepherd lying at his feet. A woman with red hair sat in a chair with a red-haired Pomeranian on her lap. The woman bent down to kiss the top of her dog's head.

"Look!" Maya nudged Kat and Grace.

The woman's hair was exactly the same colour as her dog's hair!

"Do you think she dyed her hair to get it that colour?" Maya whispered.

"Or she found exactly the right Pomeranian to match her hair," Kat whispered back.

Grace giggled.

The door of the grooming studio opened

and Aunt Jenn came striding out. She wore her light-blue grooming coat and her dangly puppy earrings. Beside her was a young man holding a boxer puppy in his arms. The man's T-shirt was wet but he was smiling.

"Thanks for clipping Porter's nails and showing me how to give him a bath," the man said. "Maybe next time he'll be a little more calm."

Aunt Jenn laughed. "I'm sure he will."

Porter barked cheerfully. He wiggled his rear end and shook his head.

"Or maybe not." Aunt Jenn grinned.

Porter's owner paid his bill and left.

"Hello, Kitty-Kat!" Aunt Jenn said. This was her special nickname for Kat. "Hello, Maya and Grace! Thank you for coming."

She turned to the two customers who were waiting.

"I'll be with you in a moment," said Aunt Jenn.

"First I must introduce my helpers to their new student! Follow me, girls."

Grace shot Kat and Maya a puzzled look. "Student?"

Kat shrugged. "Don't know," she said. "Aunt Jenn hasn't told me anything about this puppy. Let's go and find out!"

CHAPTER TWO

The girls hurried after Aunt Jenn into the doggy-daycare room. Aunt Jenn's main business was grooming dogs. She was not really prepared to board too many dogs yet. But a few times, customers had asked her for help. They didn't want to leave their puppies in a large kennel. They needed somewhere special for them to stay. Aunt Jenn could never say no to a puppy in need.

Aunt Jenn lived in an apartment above the salon. When she had a puppy boarder, she looked after him at night. Kat and her friends helped out after school and on weekends.

"Come and meet Piper," said Aunt Jenn. "She's a four-month-old Bernese mountain dog."

There were four large dog kennels along one wall of the room. Three were empty. The one under the window was not. Inside was a

beautiful, stocky puppy. She was mostly jet black but she had a rust-coloured spot above each eye. Her legs were rust-coloured but her paws were white. Her chest and throat were white. She had a white blaze between her eyes. It ran right down to her white muzzle.

When the puppy saw the girls, she jumped up and wagged her tail. The tip of her tail was white, too.

"Oh, she's gorgeous!" cried Maya.

"Hello, Piper!" said Kat. "Look at you! You're a beauty!"

Piper wagged her tail even more energetically. She smiled up at the girls.

Aunt Jenn grinned. "Piper is here for a special reason. Her owner, Greta Barlow, is preparing Piper for her first puppy show."

"But you said Piper is only four months old," said Grace. "Isn't that too young to be in a show?"

"It's very young," Aunt Jenn agreed. "That's why Greta is showing Piper in the baby puppy class. The judge looks to see how well the puppies match up to the qualities of their breed. The dog show is this Saturday at the fairgrounds."

Kat grinned. "That sounds like fun!"

"It will be Piper's first time in the ring. Greta wants Piper to get used to the hustle and bustle of a dog show. She doesn't expect Piper to win, but she wants her puppy to behave nicely," Aunt Jenn said. "Greta works from home, and she has begun to do some simple training with her every day."

Kat looked at Piper. The puppy sat in the kennel looking up at Aunt Jenn. It was almost like she was listening to her talk!

"But this week Greta must go out to see clients every day. She is very, very busy," said Aunt Jenn. "I agreed she could bring Piper here every afternoon. I told her that you girls would play with Piper and keep her company. But Greta asked if you could practise her commands with her, too. The dog show is in five days!"

Kat's eyes lit up. "Sure we will!" she said. Her heart was pounding with excitement.

Maya and Grace nodded. "We'd love to!"

"Wonderful!" said Aunt Jenn. She did a little cha-cha-cha with her feet. "I knew I could count on you!"

She spun around to Kat. "And now, I'll give you a quick demonstration of what Piper needs to practise. Can you get her out of the kennel? I'll get her leash."

Kat opened the door to the kennel and let Piper out. "Here we go, puppy," she whispered softly, taking Piper into her arms. Piper wriggled with joy. She thumped her tail.

"You're a sweetie," Kat murmured. She breathed in the lovely puppy smell. She stroked Piper's back and gave the puppy a quick kiss on the top of her head.

"Here, Piper!" called Maya. Piper trotted over to Maya and then Grace to say hello.

"She's very friendly," said Aunt Jenn. "Bernese mountain dogs are usually affectionate and calm. They are eager to please!"

After Grace and Maya patted the puppy, Piper bounded over to greet Aunt Jenn. Aunt Jenn took some dog treats from a bag on a shelf. She clipped a red leash to Piper's collar.

"Okay, Piper," said Aunt Jenn. "Let's show them what you can do! First, sitting."

Aunt Jenn held a treat in her hand. She put her arm down at her side. Aunt Jenn waited until she had Piper's attention. She turned her hand so her palm faced Piper. Slowly, she raised her hand above Piper's nose. Her thumb held the treat in place. To keep her eyes on the treat, Piper had to lift her chin very high. She had to lift her head so high that her bum went down. She sat.

"Well done, Piper!" cried the girls. Aunt Jenn gave Piper the treat. The puppy wagged her tail and gobbled up the biscuit.

"But why don't you tell Piper to *sit* while you do that?" asked Maya.

"Good question," Aunt Jenn said. "Puppies can only concentrate on one thing at a time when they are this young. So it's best to do just one command, either hand or voice. Since puppies are much better with hand movements than with words, many people do hands only. After puppies learn the hand command, trainers add in the words. The puppies learn to connect the word *sit* with the hand movement for *sit*. After that all they need is the voice command alone."

"Wow," said Maya, shaking her head. "Dog Psychology 101! This is complicated!"

Piper was standing, wagging her tail. She was looking at Aunt Jenn's pocket. That's where the other treats were waiting.

"Next," Aunt Jenn said, "Piper needs to walk nicely on a leash. Keep the leash not too loose and not too tight." Aunt Jenn held her arm out from her side. She walked Piper around the room twice. As she walked, Aunt Jenn gave Piper treats. "See how this keeps Piper paying attention to me, with her head up?"

"Nice, Piper!" said Kat, clapping.

"Next, Piper needs to hold a standing position

calmly while she is being touched," Aunt Jenn
explained. She stood in front of Piper with a
treat in her hand. She held her hand just high
enough so that Piper's neck and head were up
nicely. Her ears were perked. "Maya, can you
pat Piper, please?"

Maya reached down and stroked Piper's back.
Aunt Jenn tried to give Piper treats, but Piper
squiggled and wiggled. She licked Maya's hand.

Maya laughed. "Well, that definitely needs some work!"

"And finally, she needs to let us check her teeth." Aunt Jenn bent down and gently opened Piper's mouth. Piper wagged her tail happily.

"Easy-peasy. And that's it," said Aunt Jenn. She glanced at her watch. "Oh my goodness! Gotta go! Customers waiting! Can you take it from here, girls?"

"You bet," said Kat, as Aunt Jenn handed her the leash.

"Come and get me if you need anything." With a wave over her shoulder, Aunt Jenn was gone.

CHAPTER THREE

Kat, Maya and Grace looked at one another. Piper sat on her haunches, looking up at them.

"Hey, let's play with Piper for a little first. Get to know her a bit. Then we'll do the training," Kat suggested quickly.

"Yes!" Maya cried. "You read my mind, Kat-nip!"

"Me, too!" said Grace.

The girls sank to their knees. Piper wagged her tail happily and tried to climb into Kat's lap.

"Oh, Piper, you are so sweet!" Kat hugged Piper. She stroked the puppy's silky ears. She looked at her little socks, one on each foot. Even her little black nose was cute.

Grace was looking longingly at the puppy.

"Here, Grace. You have a turn," Kat said. Piper wiggled excitedly as Kat handed the leash to her friend.

"Oh, Piper. You are gorgeous," said Grace. "You're big too, and soft, like a big teddy bear!" She kneeled down and hugged Piper.

"Actually, an adult male Bernese mountain dog can weigh up to fifty-five kilograms," said Kat. "That's about . . ." She stopped and thought. "That's about how much my brother Aidan weighs!"

Kat's brother, Aidan, was in grade seven. He was tall and lanky, and loved playing basketball almost as much as he loved listening to music.

"Your turn," Grace told Maya with a sigh. She

kissed Piper's head and handed the leash to Maya.

"Look at these eyes," said Maya, crouching down to gaze into Piper's face. "Deep brown. They are so beautiful."

Piper seemed to like that compliment. She gave Maya's chin a sloppy kiss.

"Nice one, Piper," Maya said, laughing. "And here's one back at you." She kissed the puppy's head. "I think I like Bernese mountain dogs," she said. "But it's such an odd name, isn't it? *Bernese mountain dog.*"

"These dogs came from a mountainous area in the middle of Switzerland," said Kat. "The area is called Bern, so the dogs are called Bernese mountain dogs."

"There we go," Maya said. She made googly eyes at Kat. "Of course you would know this."

Maya turned to Piper. "This girl is the Einstein of the dog world!" she told the puppy. Piper wagged her tail, loving the attention.

Kat made googly eyes back at Maya. "And that's not all," she said. "Piper's ancestors were big, strong working dogs. They helped out on the farm by pulling carts. They could pull up to ten times their own weight. That would be like one Bernese mountain dog pulling ten others."

"Did you read *Dog Breeds of the World* last night?" Grace asked.

"For the twenty-first time?" teased Maya.

Kat grinned. She was trying to learn as much about dogs as she could. That's why she spent hours reading about dogs on the Internet. That's why her favourite book was *Dog Breeds of the World*. Maya always kidded her about it. She said Kat had probably read the book twenty-one times. But Kat knew it was more like one hundred times!

"Okay, teddy bear. Off you go," said Maya. She unclipped the leash. At once, the puppy ran off to explore the room. She found the basket of dog toys. She poked her nose in them. When a chewy toy fell out of the basket, she pushed at it with her nose. She poked her nose in the basket again and a plush toy fell out. Gently, Piper picked it up.

"Nice choice," said Maya, laughing.

The puppy trotted across the room with it. She held it while she investigated the other empty kennels. She held it while she sniffed at the desk and chair that stood against the wall. Finally she sat down. She made growling sounds. She dropped the toy. She sprang forward and picked it up again. She tossed her head from side to side.

"She is so adorable," said Grace.

Grace waited until Piper dropped the toy again. Then Grace picked it up and threw it across the room. "Go get it!" she told Piper.

But Piper didn't budge. Instead she began to tug on Grace's pant legs. "Hey, don't do that!" Grace said. Then she said, more firmly, "No, Piper."

Piper looked at Grace and tilted her head. But she still held the pant leg in her teeth.

Maya laughed. "It's like she's saying, 'Oh, come on, please?'"

"Here, Piper. Have your toy," suggested Kat. She went and picked up the plush toy that Grace had thrown for the puppy. She offered it to Piper. The puppy dropped Grace's pant leg and pounced on the toy.

"Good one, Kat," said Grace.

For a while, the girls took turns picking up Piper's favourite toy when she dropped it. They threw it across the room. Now the puppy chased after it. The girls asked her to bring it back, but she wouldn't. Not once.

"I feel like I'm getting as much exercise as Piper," said Grace, as she went to pick up the toy one more time.

Maya laughed. "These dogs are totally not retrievers," she said.

Finally Kat said, "Okay. Time for some puppy training?"

Grace and Maya agreed. They each took a handful of dog treats. They decided to practise the commands in the order Aunt Jenn had shown them.

First they took turns asking Piper to sit. Piper did well. Not right away, but after a few times.

Then they took turns walking her on the leash. Each girl pretended to be a judge, touching her and then checking her mouth. Maya walked her around the room twice. Then Grace did. And then Kat.

At first Piper just wanted to play. But soon she settled down. When the "judge" came to touch her, she looked for her treat. She stood calmly. As the judge opened Piper's mouth, the puppy wagged her tail.

But soon Piper began to yawn. She lay down while Kat was walking her.

"Come on, Piper," Kat said firmly. "Let's go."

Piper wouldn't move.

Maya giggled. "I think she's exhausted."

Piper yawned again. "I think you're right,"

said Kat with a grin.

It was time for the girls to head home.

Reluctantly the girls put Piper back in her kennel. She wagged her tail and curled up in a ball. She gave one more yawn and closed her eyes.

"See you tomorrow, Piper," said Kat.

"Bye, Piper," said Maya.

CHAPTER FOUR

The next day, Tuesday, Maya, Kat and Grace arrived at Tails Up right after school. Tony flagged them down as they entered the waiting room.

"Ladies," he said, "Jenn, groomer extraordinaire, bestest boss ever, wonders if you might like to take Piper to the park today. She said it would be good for the puppy to practise her moves outdoors in a new environment."

"Great idea!" said Kat enthusiastically. "Thanks, Tony."

Grace stroked Marmalade's head. Marmalade twitched her whiskers in delight, but she refused to look at Grace.

"This cat is too good for us mere humans," said Tony, with a grin. Grace giggled.

When they entered the doggy-daycare room, Piper sprang to her feet and wagged her tail. The girls threw down their backpacks. Maya hurried over and let Piper out of the kennel.

"You sweet, sweet girl," cooed Maya. "Did you miss us? We missed you!"

"Look," said Kat. "Here's a note for us."

On the side of the kennel was an envelope with "To Kat, Maya and Grace" written on the outside. Kat opened it. She read it aloud: *"Hello, girls! Piper told me how lovely the three of you are. She said you are good teachers and she is happy you are helping to train her! Thank you! From Greta."*

Grace and Maya laughed. "We like you, too!" Maya said to Piper, giving her a hug and kissing the top of her head.

Kat clipped the leash onto Piper's collar and off they went. Piper only rested a few times on the way to the park. When they got there, she was full of pep!

Grace's new house was on one of the streets that ran beside the park. One end of the park was a playground. At the other end was a hill with a grove of trees on top.

Kat had lived in Orchard Valley all her life, and she had been coming to the park ever since she could remember. The grove on top of the hill was Kat's favourite place. From up there she could see the town on one side and the countryside on the other. Along the sides of the park were several rows of trees and bushes.

The girls decided to play with Piper first, like at Tails Up. They ran back and forth across the

park with her several times until Piper had used up some of her boundless puppy energy. Now she would be more calm and more likely to listen to them.

Then it was time to do the training activities.

This time, Grace went first, asking Piper to sit, walking her, then asking her to stand nicely. Maya went next. Piper did well.

"Your turn, Kat," said Maya cheerfully. She handed the leash to Kat.

"Thanks, Maya," Kat said. Then she took a deep breath. *Ready, set, go.*

Kat did the hand movements for *sit*. Piper sat once, twice, three times.

"Good girl!" said Kat, pleased.

She began to walk Piper in a big circle on the grass. Now Kat noticed a boy leaning against a tree, watching. She guessed he was about eleven years old. Beside him, sitting patiently, was a black and tan dachshund.

Kat continued. She gave Piper treats as she walked. But when Piper saw the other dog, she wagged her tail. She tried to go and say hello.

"No, Piper," said Kat. "Come on. We're not done yet."

She continued walking the circle, but Piper was not looking up at her anymore. Her attention was on the dachshund.

Kat stopped in front of Maya and Grace. She tried to encourage Piper to stand nicely while

Grace stroked her and looked at her teeth, but Piper wiggled and waggled.

"It's that boy," said Kat, annoyed. "That boy and his dog. Piper keeps looking at them."

Maya shrugged. "Well, that's why your aunt said we should come here. To get Piper used to distractions."

But why did it have to happen when *she* was

training Piper? Just when Piper was beginning to listen to her.

"That boy is coming over," pointed out Grace.

Kat frowned. She gave up trying to make Piper listen.

The dachshund was not on a leash. He came right up to Piper on his short little legs, wagging his tail. Piper lay flat on the grass, waiting for the older dog to approach.

The dachshund sniffed Piper all over. Then he gave Piper a friendly lick on the nose. Piper rolled onto her back. She wanted to play.

"You know, anyone can show a nice-looking dog," the boy said, as he came near. "It's another thing to be tested on obedience."

The three girls exchanged annoyed glances.

"Watch," the boy ordered. At first Kat thought he was speaking to his dog, but then she realized the boy was speaking to them.

"Baxter," the boy said. The dachshund lifted

his head and looked at the boy. The boy made a hand signal. At once the dog came and stood beside his leg. He looked at the boy intently.

The boy made another hand signal. Baxter ran across the grass toward the trees, his short legs a blur, his long ears flapping. When he got there he looked at the boy again. The boy made a gesture. Baxter turned and weaved through the trees, this way and that.

Again, the dachshund looked at the boy. The boy made another hand signal. Baxter jumped over some branches lying on the ground. One and then another. A hand signal and Baxter wove through the trees again, and then he was galloping back toward the boy.

When Baxter reached him, he sat down and waited, looking happily up at the boy's face. The boy reached into his pocket and gave the dachshund a treat.

Despite herself, Kat was impressed. "Nice,"

she said. "Baxter is a star!"

Maya and Grace nodded. "He's great," they agreed.

"I know. He could probably win a competition without me," bragged the boy. He gave Baxter another treat.

"This is Maya and Grace, my friends," said Kat. "And I'm Kat."

"My name's Robert," said the boy. "There's a dog show this weekend. I'm showing Baxter in the obedience class. I'm a junior handler in the intermediate class. Obviously."

"Obviously," said Maya. She looked at Kat and Grace and raised her eyebrows. None of them knew what a junior handler was. None of them was going to admit it.

"So, see you," said Robert.

"Bye, Baxter." Grace gave the dachshund a final pat. Baxter gave a little wag of the tail. Robert turned and walked away.

CHAPTER FIVE

The next afternoon the girls took Piper to the park again.

"Let's follow the same routine as yesterday," Maya suggested.

Kat and Grace agreed. First they played with Piper. She had great fun running with them across the field. This time they took in the playground too. They led her through the cement tunnel. They held her while they rode on the seesaw. They encouraged her to walk along the wooden stumps and then leap from rock to rock in the rock garden.

"You are such a good sport, Piper!" Kat praised her.

Then it was time for the training activities.

"Why don't you go first this time, Kat?" Grace suggested. "Remember how tired Piper got when it was your turn yesterday?"

"Okay," said Kat gratefully. *Maybe Piper will do better with me this time,* she thought.

Like always, Kat first asked Piper to sit. She held the dog treat in her hand. She lifted her hand, palm out, in front of the Bernese puppy. Piper wagged her tail. She turned away.

Once. Twice. Three times. Each time Kat made the same motion. Each time Piper wagged her tail and turned away. She pulled toward the trees.

"Piper," Kat snapped. She put her hands

on her hips. "Pay attention! You're not behaving properly."

When Piper heard Kat's angry tone, her ears drooped. She crouched down on the ground, looking up at Kat.

Kat's anger melted away immediately. "I'm sorry, Piper," she said. "I didn't mean to frighten you." She knelt beside Piper and stroked her head. Right away the puppy jumped up and tried to climb into her lap.

Kat laughed with relief. "You forgive me already? What a sweet girl," she said.

"Try one more time," Grace suggested.

Kat did, but Piper still refused to sit. She spun around toward the trees and barked.

"It's that boy," said Maya. "Look."

Kat frowned and put her hands on her hips.

Robert and his dog, Baxter, were there. They were standing, watching. They were distracting Piper. That had to be the problem.

"Well, I'm not going to let them interfere," said Kat.

Piper wagged her tail. Her eyes were sparkling. She wanted to play with Baxter. But Kat held the leash firmly, her arm out. She waited until the puppy was still. Then she said, "Let's go, girl," and she began to walk with her. As she walked she tried to give Piper treats from her pocket.

Piper pulled toward Baxter. But Kat continued, refusing to let Piper say hello to the dachshund. She tried to stay calm but it was difficult.

When Kat and Piper completed the circle, Maya stepped forward. "Good work. Now I'll be the judge," she told Kat.

"Okay," Kat agreed. She knelt beside Piper. She put a treat in her hand and held it out in front of the puppy. Piper lunged for the treat.

Maya shook her head. "You'd get a big, fat zero for this type of behaviour, Piper," she said in her stern judge voice.

"Let's try again," said Kat. She walked Piper around and then stopped. She placed each of Piper's little white paws just so. She patted Piper. Again Kat put her hand out in front of Piper with a treat in her palm. The puppy stood perfectly still for three seconds. Then she lunged for the treat.

"Okay, time to call it quits for today!" Kat decided. "I'm out of patience. And I think Piper is, too!"

Grace looked concerned. "Are you sure you don't want to try one more time?" Grace asked. "I know you can do it."

"No, I'm sure," said Kat, sighing.

Suddenly the black and tan dachshund was there, greeting Piper. Piper lay down, wagging her tail happily. Once Baxter licked her nose, Piper jumped to her feet. Even though she wasn't close to being full-grown yet, she was bigger than the friendly dachshund. The older dog stood patiently as the puppy nipped playfully at him.

Kat heard Robert call, "Baxter!"

Instantly the dachshund's attention focused on Robert. The boy made a signal. The girls watched as Baxter turned and raced back toward Robert. Then the boy raised his hand

and made a different signal. The dachshund stopped abruptly and sat still halfway across the field. A few long moments passed. Baxter didn't move.

Then another signal and Baxter turned and ran a big arc around the field, looping back toward Robert.

Piper watched too, wagging her tail.

"See, Piper?" Maya said. "Now there's a pro."

"One day you'll be able to do that too, Piper," said Grace confidently.

Kat knelt beside the puppy and held her close. She stroked Piper's silky ears and breathed in her beautiful puppy smell.

She knew Piper could learn to do anything.

But what about me? Kat wondered. *Maybe I'm just not good enough to help train you.*

CHAPTER SIX

"Only two more days to the show!" Grace said. It was Thursday and the three girls and Piper were off to the park again.

Grace sounded excited, but Kat was worried.

"What if Piper doesn't listen to Greta on Saturday? Piper seems to co-operate with you two, but when I try . . . Maybe I'm *untraining* Piper!" Kat had worried about it all last night. She had worried about it all day at school. She had gone over and over the way she had held Piper's leash, the way she had moved her hand, the way she had . . .

Then again, maybe it wasn't her fault at all. Maybe it was that boy's fault. And his dog. They had been distracting Piper . . .

"Don't be silly, Kat-nip," said Maya, poking Kat's arm. "You're not doing anything wrong. Piper is just . . . temperamental. Like me!"

"Temperamental?" asked Grace. She was holding Piper's leash. The Bernese mountain dog pup was trotting along beside the girls.

"You know. *Sensitive*," said Maya in her drawling actress voice. She flung her arms out dramatically. "*Moody*." She made a pouting face, then she made a happy face. Then she spun around and around, flapping her arms like wings. "*Unpredictable*," she cried.

Kat and Grace laughed. And then they laughed even harder because Piper had stopped in her

tracks. She was staring at Maya.

"That's right, Piper. You and me, pup. Sensitive, moody," Maya repeated, "and unpredictable."

Maya spun around once more, and Piper took cover behind Grace. The girls laughed as the pup peeked her nose out from between Grace's legs.

"Oh, Piper," said Kat, reassuringly. She patted

the puppy's head. "It's okay. That's just Maya being dramatic!"

In a moment the puppy was bounding along beside them again.

When they reached the park, they ran across the field with the puppy. They ran all the way to the top of the hill and then they turned and ran down.

When they got to the bottom, Piper looked up at them expectantly. The girls laughed. "You want to do it again?" asked Kat.

"Piper, you are so much fun!" said Grace.

Up they ran again and then down.

"Okay, time for your training," announced Maya.

Grace went first. Kat had mixed feelings. Part of her hoped Grace didn't do well with Piper just so she wouldn't be the only one having trouble. The other part of her wanted Grace and the puppy to do well.

Piper was calm and she listened nicely.

The puppy was the same with Maya.

Then it was Kat's turn.

"Keep up the good work, girls. That's what today's note from Greta said," Kat reminded Piper. Piper cocked her head to one side. She wagged her tail.

"You are agreeing, but let's see if you do what I ask you!" said Kat. Piper wagged her tail again, and Maya and Grace laughed.

Kat reached into her pocket and took out a dog treat. She did the hand movements for *sit*. Piper sat once, twice, three times. *Phew!* thought Kat.

But then, just like the other days, Kat saw that Robert was there, leaning against a tree, watching. Baxter sat beside him.

Kat set off at once with Piper, hoping that the Bernese mountain dog puppy had not noticed the boy and his dog. She held her arm out like Aunt Jenn had shown her. "Walk nicely," she said to Piper, giving her a treat as they walked.

Piper did walk nicely until they were turning to go back to the girls. That's when she saw Baxter. She was no longer interested in Kat or the treats. She began pulling toward Baxter. She wanted to say hello to her friend.

"Piper, in the show there will be many other dogs. You can't visit with them whenever you want," Kat told her. "Your job in the show is to let the judge see what a well-trained puppy you are. You have to walk and move nicely, not pull toward the other dogs and wag your tail."

Piper cocked her head and listened, but when Kat tried to walk on with her, the puppy wanted to go to Baxter.

Kat glared at Robert. Did he really have to stand there with Baxter and watch? Couldn't he see that he was causing her problems?

And now he and Baxter were coming their way. He was going to make it even more difficult.

"Piper has to get used to other dogs being around," said Robert as he approached. "It's good practice for her."

Kat glared at him. Easy for him to say with the dog who could do anything. "Can't you just leave us alone?" she complained.

It was as if Robert had not heard. And the closer Baxter got, the more Piper pulled toward the dachshund.

"Baxter was like this, too," Robert said. "A

puppy has to learn to listen to you alone when she is training."

But Piper wasn't listening — not at all. Kat wanted to give up. What did it matter now? Piper wasn't co-operating anyway.

"Go on," Robert said. Finally he had stopped coming closer. He made a motion, and Baxter sat beside him. "Keep trying."

"But I don't know what to do," Kat burst out. Her eyes were stinging. *Do not cry,* she ordered herself. *Not in front of this terrible boy.* "Can't you just go away? You and Baxter?"

Robert shook his head. "No," he said. "Piper has to learn that she needs to do what you say above all else. Just keep doing what you've been doing. Show Piper that you are continuing with the training."

Kat blinked. She took a deep breath. "Okay, Piper. Listen. I'm the trainer, and I say we can do this. We're going to finish our circle."

Piper looked at Kat and cocked her head.

Kat lifted her hand, signalling Piper to sit. Piper sat.

Kat took out some dog treats and put them in her hand. She held Piper's leash just as Aunt Jenn had shown her. "Okay, walk nicely now, Piper," she said.

Piper turned her head to look at Baxter but she walked beside Kat. Soon she was looking up at Kat, paying attention to her and eating the treats.

When Kat arrived back at the start of her circle, she was bursting with happiness. Piper had listened to her the whole way. She had been calm and obedient — despite all the distractions.

"Well done," said Grace.

"Nice!" said Maya, clapping her hands. "But what did that boy say? Was he bothering you?"

"No," Kat said. "He was actually . . ." Kat looked around to see Robert's reaction. But he and Baxter were gone. " . . . trying to be helpful."

Kat was surprised to feel a twinge of disappointment that Robert had not seen how well Piper had behaved.

Then came another thought. Maybe Piper behaved so nicely *because* Robert and Baxter had left. Maybe it had nothing to do with Piper getting used to other dogs being around. Maybe Kat had not really helped teach Piper much at all.

CHAPTER SEVEN

"Tomorrow is Saturday, the big day," said Maya. She, Grace and Kat waved hello to Tony and headed into the doggy-daycare room at Tails Up.

"Yes, it will be showtime for you, Piper!" Kat announced. The puppy stood in the kennel watching them and wagging her tail.

Grace hurried to let Piper out of the kennel. Kat took the note from the envelope on the kennel. "Greta says, *Please just play with Piper today. No training. She gets a day off before her debut tomorrow! Hope to see all three of you at the show. 11:30. Ring D. Come early and say hello. And thanks for all your help!"*

Grace clapped her hands together. "I'm so excited to see the show and to meet Greta! I hope Piper does well!" she said.

"Me, too!" Maya said. "It's been really fun to help out."

Kat didn't say anything. She couldn't really tell her friends that training Piper had not been much fun for her, could she?

When they got to the park, the girls ran back and forth across the field a few times with Piper. They all climbed up the hill and looked out over the countryside. When they were rested, they all ran back down again.

This time Kat had remembered to bring her camera. She took several photos of Piper to add to the Puppy Collection. It was a special scrapbook that she, Maya and Grace were creating. The girls drew pictures and wrote about each breed of puppy that they liked. They were including all the puppies they helped look after at Tails Up. They wanted to include Piper, too.

Kat took a photo of Piper bounding across the field with her tail held high. She took a photo of Grace lying on the grass with Piper leaping about on her tummy. She took a photo of Maya with her arms around Piper, their smiling faces side by side. Then Grace took a photo of Piper licking Kat's face.

The whole time, Kat kept expecting to see Robert and Baxter at the park. Yesterday she had felt angry at him, then almost grateful. Today she wasn't quite sure how she felt. Everything was all mixed up inside her.

The girls took Piper back to Tails Up and said a special goodbye.

"But we'll see you and Greta tomorrow at the show," Maya told Piper.

"And we know you'll have a really good time," said Grace.

Kat was the last to hold Piper. "Good luck," she whispered in the puppy's ear, before she let Piper back into her kennel. "See you at the show!"

Maya and Grace walked with Kat to her house. She had invited them for dinner. After they ate they all worked together on the Puppy Collection.

Kat drew pictures of Piper while Maya and Grace wrote up a description of the puppy.

"Okay, let me read it out," said Maya. "Kat, let us know what you think. *Piper is a Bernese mountain dog. She is four months old. She is like a beautiful big teddy bear. She is training to be a show dog. She is learning to walk nicely on the leash. She is very friendly and she has a beautiful smile!*"

"Perfect," said Kat.

"Let's leave some room on the page," said Grace, pointing. "We can add the photos we took today once we print them out."

"And let's leave a spot for the photo we'll take

of Piper at the show tomorrow!" said Maya.

The show! How would Piper do? Kat couldn't wait to find out. She couldn't wait to cheer on the sweet puppy while she showed in the ring for the very first time.

CHAPTER EIGHT

It was wonderful. There were dogs everywhere! Big dogs, small dogs, young dogs, old dogs, dogs of every colour. Kat, Maya and Grace couldn't stop grinning.

Kat's mother had dropped off the girls at the Orchard Valley fairgrounds at ten o'clock. She was coming back to pick them up at twelve thirty. Kat's brother, Aidan, was there, too. He had agreed to keep an eye on the girls.

The dog show was held in a large indoor arena. The girls wandered happily through the building, admiring all the dogs. Aidan trailed after them.

A woman was putting a top knot in her poodle's hair. A Shih Tzu yawned while two serious-looking men hurried to put bows in his hair. Some dogs were being groomed, others were being bathed.

"Look!" Maya whispered. A competitor was blow-drying the hair on a wet Havanese. Grace and Kat giggled.

The girls stopped at one ring to watch part of an agility trial. They watched a border collie being guided around a course by its handler. The dog jumped over a wall, ran along a seesaw, climbed up a ramp and scooted through a tunnel.

In another ring, they saw ten German shepherds lined up. The judge was looking at them one by one.

"I really like dog shows," sighed Grace happily.

"Me, too," agreed Maya.

"Oh, I almost forgot. I have a joke for you!" Kat said.

"Oh no," Maya groaned. "I thought we might avoid your terrible torture today."

Grace grinned. "Uh-oh."

Kat made a face. "Well, I'm going to tell it anyway," she said. "What is it called when a cat wins a dog show?"

But just then, before the girls could answer, the last part of an announcement caught Kat's attention. " . . . *competition for junior handlers eleven and up will begin in Ring A at eleven fifteen.*"

"Eleven and up. That might be the event that Robert and Baxter are in," said Kat.

"Maybe," said Maya, with a shrug. "Hey, I saw a sign saying the puppies are this way. Come on. Let's go find Greta and Piper. We don't want to miss seeing them before Piper's event."

Kat hesitated. "I'd like to find Robert," she

said. "I'd like to wish him good luck."

"Really?" Maya asked, frowning.

"Good idea, Kat," said Grace quickly. She put a hand on Maya's arm. "If we hurry, we can do both. We say hello to Robert and see Piper before she goes into the ring."

Kat explained everything to Aidan while Maya quickly asked an official for directions. They had to leave the building and go all the way across the fairgrounds to a smaller arena.

"We'll have to run to make it back in time," said Aidan, glancing at his watch. "Maybe we shouldn't try."

"Oh, we can do it," said Kat. "Right, Grace? Maya? Come on! Hurry!"

The girls were panting by the time they reached the arena. There were three rings inside, and they followed a sign to Ring A.

"There he is," said Grace, pointing. "There's Robert."

Robert and three other young handlers waited outside Ring A with their dogs. Each was nicely dressed and wore an arm band with a competitor number on it. One had a poodle, one had a sheltie and one had a Labrador retriever. The other handlers looked quite a bit older than Robert, maybe thirteen or fourteen, Kat thought. They were smiling and chatting with each other. But not Robert. He stood apart with Baxter at his feet. His face was pale. He was biting his lip.

"He doesn't look too good," said Maya.

"Let's go and talk to him," said Kat.

Aidan pointed to Ring B. "I'll be right there, watching the agility competition."

"Okay," Kat agreed.

The girls hurried up to Robert and Baxter.

"Robert," said Kat. "Are you okay?"

Robert didn't even pretend to smile. "My parents were supposed to come, but they couldn't. My older brother dropped me off here,

late. He's parking the car. I don't know if he'll get back in time to watch me." His voice shook. "It's my first time showing in this older category"

Maya and Grace exchanged a worried glance. But Kat said, "Robert, you'll be fine."

"I think I'm the youngest in this group," he

said softly. "I think I've changed my mind. I don't want to compete."

Kat shot a desperate look at Maya and Grace. The girls looked back at her helplessly.

Then Baxter whined. He thumped his tail on the ground. And suddenly Kat had an idea.

"Robert," she said. "Remember what you said in the park? You said Baxter could win the competition by himself. Right?"

Robert didn't respond for a minute. Then he looked down at his dachshund. "Right," he said. "I did say that."

Baxter wagged his tail enthusiastically.

"Piper is in the show today with her owner. She's the one who might have trouble. Remember how she was with me?" Kat laughed. "She was so distracted! She wouldn't do anything I asked! She's just a puppy."

Robert nodded.

"But Baxter's a pro," Kat continued, "and

70

you can't let him down. He needs you to be confident. He needs you to take him in the ring and show everyone how well trained he is."

Baxter wagged his tail again.

"Look, Baxter is trying to tell you the same thing!" Kat said.

Robert didn't answer for a moment. Then he nodded slowly. "You're right," he said. "My brother's not here, but that's okay. I can't let Baxter down."

He kneeled beside Baxter and scratched him under the chin.

"So, Kat," said Maya. She pointed to the clock on the wall. "It's eleven ten. Piper's event is about to begin. We've already missed meeting Greta before the event." She turned to Robert. "We have to watch our puppy perform now, Robert. But good luck to you and Baxter!"

"Yes, good luck," said Grace.

Robert tried to smile. Then he buried his face in Baxter's coat.

"Okay, come on, Kat," urged Maya.

More than anything, Kat wanted to watch Piper compete. She had been waiting for this all week. But she knew she couldn't just leave Robert here alone. Robert and Baxter needed her help. She knew Piper would understand.

"You two go ahead," Kat spoke quietly to Maya and Grace. "I'm going to stay here with Robert."

"But, Kat," protested Grace. "Are you sure?"

"You're going to miss seeing Piper in her first show? You're going to miss that just for this boy, who we hardly even know?" Maya said.

"Yes," Kat said quickly. "Just make sure you memorize every single detail about Piper's performance. Every single one. And don't forget to take some photos. We can add them to Piper's pages in the Puppy Collection."

Grace and Maya hesitated. Kat saw they felt badly about leaving her.

But she insisted, "It's okay. And Aidan will stay with me. Please. Just hurry so you don't miss the event, too!"

Maya shook her head. "You are too good to be true," she teased Kat.

Grace gave her a quick hug.

Kat watched as her two friends hurried over to speak with Aidan. He pointed to his watch and nodded.

As Maya and Grace ran for the exit, Kat couldn't help feeling her heart sink.

CHAPTER NINE

Kat pictured Piper's beautiful black face with the brilliant white streak. How would the puppy do in the ring? Had their training helped Piper at all? It was difficult not to run and catch up to Maya and Grace. It was difficult not to be able to watch Piper perform. *Did I make the right decision?* Kat wondered.

An announcement sounded: *"Junior competitors in the Intermediate Novice class, please enter Ring A."*

Robert stood up. "That's Baxter and me," he said. "Hey, you should catch up with your friends," he told Kat, pointing at them.

"It's okay," Kat said. "I'm going to stay here."

Robert stared at her.

"Really?" he asked. "Are you sure?"

Kat nodded. "Yup," she said. "Now go in there and let Baxter show his stuff!"

Robert straightened his shoulders. He grinned at Baxter and said, "Okay, it's showtime!" Kat knew she had made the right decision.

Robert followed the other three handlers into the ring. Kat went over to the railing. She stood beside the other spectators. She realized she had butterflies in her stomach!

The judge walked across the ring then turned and walked back.

"The 'heeling' exercise is first."

Kat jumped. The teenage boy who had just pushed in beside her at the railing began speaking.

"The handlers have to follow that path as their dogs walk nicely at their heels."

Kat frowned. It was rude of him to push his way in.

Then the boy pointed at Robert. "That's my brother, Robbie," he said proudly. "And that's our dog, Baxter!"

Kat's mouth dropped open. "You're Robert's brother?" she said.

"Yes," he replied. "You know Robbie? You're a friend of his?"

Kat paused to wonder. Was she Robert's friend? She made up her mind. "Yes," she said. "I am. I'm Kat."

"I'm Daniel, and I'm late. Had trouble parking. Then I went into the wrong arena and got all turned around." He looked worried. "Robbie just moved up into this age category, so he's the youngest. I know he'll be nervous."

"But Baxter is so well trained," said Kat.

"Won't he do well?"

"Probably, but in a junior handler competition, it's not really the dog that's being judged. It's mostly the handler who gets the points," Daniel explained. "Three-quarters of the score is for the handler. Only one-quarter is for the dog's performance. If Robbie is too nervous, he could really end up doing badly."

"Oh!" said Kat. "I didn't know that!" Her butterflies got even worse.

The judge went over to Robert and Baxter.

"They judge the dogs in order of their size," Daniel said. "Baxter is the smallest in this group, so he and Robert will probably go first."

Sure enough, Robert made a signal to the dachshund. Then the pair set off.

"The handler has to be calm and quiet. He can't talk or snap his fingers unless it's necessary. And the dog has to wait until he's told what to do before he moves," Daniel explained quietly.

77

Baxter walked nicely beside Robert on a loose leash. Three times Robert stopped. Baxter did too. When Robert changed speeds, Baxter did too. Robert finished up right where the judge had finished.

Two other officials came into the ring. They stopped part-way down the ring on each side. Robert walked Baxter around them in a figure eight pattern.

"Nice work. Baxter isn't at all distracted by the officials," Daniel said quietly. "Look how Robbie doesn't look at Baxter while he walks. He can count on him being right there, just at his heel." Daniel was holding the rail tightly. *He's nervous too!* Kat thought.

When the walking exercise was done, the judge came over to Baxter. He touched the dachshund's head, shoulders and hindquarters. Baxter stood very still.

Then Robert and Baxter did another walking

exercise, but this time Robert unclipped Baxter from the leash. Baxter moved beside Robert like his shadow, slowing down and stopping when the boy did.

"Good," Daniel said. "Now the recall. First

Robbie asks Baxter to stay. Then he'll call Baxter to come to him."

Kat saw Robert make a signal to Baxter. The dachshund trotted straight to Robert and sat down in front of him.

Kat grinned. Baxter and Robert were doing so well!

Next, the other three competitors did the same routine. The handler of the Labrador retriever did well. But to Kat, the handlers of the sheltie and the poodle seemed nervous. Each had to signal more than once to convince their dogs to sit or stay.

"Do you think Robert and Baxter were the best?" Kat asked Daniel. "Did they win?"

"It's not over yet," Daniel told her. "They still have to do the group exercise."

Kat groaned. It was so suspenseful.

Now the four handlers unclipped their dogs' leashes. They placed them on the ground behind their dogs.

The judge gave the handlers instructions. The handlers signalled their dogs to sit and then walked away from them. They stood, looking at their dogs.

"The dogs have to sit still for one full minute," Daniel told Kat.

Kat could hardly breathe. "Don't move, Baxter," she whispered. "Don't move!"

After about thirty seconds, the little poodle suddenly jumped up and ran to her owner.

"Uh-oh," said Kat.

The sheltie stood up, too. Kat was certain the dog was going to run to his handler. His handler frowned. He made a signal to his dog. The sheltie sat down again.

"He'll lose some points for repeating the signal," Daniel murmured.

Finally the minute was up. Kat breathed a sigh of relief.

"Good boy!" said Daniel.

The judge asked the competitors to walk back to their dogs.

"Is it over now?" Kat asked hopefully.

"Not quite," Daniel told her. "They have to repeat the same exercise, but this time the dogs lie down for three minutes."

Again, the Labrador retriever and Baxter were the stars.

"Well done, Robert!" Daniel looked so proud of his brother. "Now all we have to do is wait for the results!"

CHAPTER TEN

Fourth place went to the poodle. Third place went to the sheltie.

Kat held her breath.

"Second place goes to Robert and Baxter," announced the judge.

Robert grinned as the judge handed him a green ribbon. He reached down and patted Baxter.

"Yahoo!" called out Daniel. Kat applauded enthusiastically.

The judge gave the first place ribbon to the Labrador retriever and his handler.

Robert came hurrying out of the ring. His face lit up when he saw Daniel. "Hey, you made it!" he said.

"Of course I did!" said Daniel slapping Robert on the back. "You and Baxter were terrific!"

"Yes, you were," said Kat, grinning.

"Thanks," said Robert. He held up the ribbon. "Second place. Baxter's amazing!" He picked up the dachshund and hugged him.

Robert looked at Kat. He said quietly, "And so are you, Kat. I don't think I could have done it without you."

"Oh, you would have been just fine," Kat said. "You and Baxter are a good team."

Just then Kat saw Aidan waving at her to come.

"I have to go now, Robert," Kat said. "Congratulations again."

"Maybe I'll see you in the park," the boy replied. Baxter barked once, twice. "Baxter and I, that is," he added, with a grin.

Kat and Aidan hurried off to find Grace and Maya. When they entered the first arena, an official pointed them toward Ring D, where the puppy class had been held.

"There they are!" Kat told Aidan.

Maya and Grace were patting the beautiful Bernese mountain puppy. A stout woman in a crisp white shirt and a black skirt was holding Piper's leash and smiling proudly.

"Kat!" cried Maya and Grace, seeing her approaching.

The woman beamed at Kat. "So you're Kat!" she said. "So nice to meet you. I'm Greta." She took Kat's hand and shook it firmly. "Piper did so well in the ring. She didn't win a ribbon, but she was calm and happy. I know she had fun!" Greta shook Kat's hand one last time. "Thank you for your help with my puppy, Kat."

"You're welcome," Kat said, pleased. She crouched beside Piper.

"Well done," she told the puppy. She stroked her soft fur. "I'm sorry I couldn't watch you in the ring, but you did such a good job."

Piper licked Kat's hand. The puppy gave Kat one of her special smiles.

Then Aidan announced that it was time to go. Greta thanked the girls again. "I'll let your aunt know when Piper is going to compete again so you can come and watch, if you like!"

As the girls hurried after Aidan, Maya and Grace told Kat more about how Piper had behaved in the ring.

"And I remembered to take some photos of her," said Maya. "We can put them in the Puppy Collection."

While they waited outside the arena for Kat's mother, Kat told the girls about Robert and Baxter's performance.

"Second place!" Grace cheered. Then she suddenly said, "Hey! The joke! Kat, you never told us the answer to your dog joke."

Kat raised her eyebrows ominously. "Are you sure you want to hear it? It will be terrible, remember."

"So true," said Maya. "However, although it's painful hearing a terrible answer, it's even worse not hearing the answer at all." She took a deep breath. "Okay, Kat-nip, spill. What happens when a cat wins a dog show?"

Kat shrugged. "Okay. You asked for it. When a cat wins a dog show, it's a catastrophe. Get it? A cat-has-trophy?"

"All-time worst joke," gasped Grace. Her lips were twitching.

"All-time worst," Maya agreed. "A record-breaker!" She made a face.

Kat pretended to look hurt.

All at once, the three girls gave up trying not

to laugh and burst out giggling. When Aidan looked over and rolled his eyes at them, Kat laughed even harder.

For more Puppy Collection fun, check out these other books in the series.

ISBN 978-1-4431-2409-6

ISBN 978-1-4431-2410-2

ISBN 978-1-4431-2411-9

ISBN 978-1-4431-3358-6